A Young Soldiers Worse Experience In Vietnam, In The Summer Of 196.

A young soldiers worse experience during his last 4 months in the summer of 1967 in Vietnam. A young soldier was out in the bush like he had been many times before patrolling. He had been in many fire fights where he was shooting into a direction that was determined the danger could be coming from. Him and all his fellow soldiers shooting in the same direction. Then it would be decided all was safe to proceed you depended on those soldiers who would determine the safety of proceeding. So you were less likely to be killed. This time he would run into the situation that would alter his life for the next 30 plus years. Unlike war movies he had seen where you confront your enemy and fight and kill them gallantly. He never knew if he had killed anyone, that was not unusual many ex-soldiers who went to Vietnam said that also. He came to an open area him and his fellow soldiers that was safe, soldiers and equipment every where. He was in a long line of soldiers waiting to move up a steep hill. Then he heard the start of shouting and screaming that would change his life instantly for more then 30 years. The sound of American soldier interrogators shouting in English and broken Vietnamese. The screams of the Vietnamese men and women crying and trying to answer the interrogators questions. Then the final sounds of screaming "No." Then the sounds of automatic weapons firing, then it stopped suddenly.

He kept advancing to the spot where he heard the sounds. Then there it was men and women, theirs bodies in a pile with bullet holes all through them. The sight that would stay in his mind for the next 30 plus years. Later he asked a fellow soldier he knew he could talk to about "What," and "Why," did that happen? The fellow soldier said they were suspected of being Vietcong forwards. They were not going to take them prisoners, and they were not going to let them go. Because if they did they would as soon as possible report to the Vietcong, the size and strength of the force they had encountered. This young soldier after his two year enlistment went home and lived his life as fully as he could. He went to VA counselors and many private veterans groups that finally helped him to let go of what was troubling him. Is not our minds incredibly fascinating that it would make us responsible for what we saw? Even though we had no part of that slaughter and murder of our fellow human beings. This story I hope pays tribute to all the individuals in every conflict we have been in. They left their ordinary lives to get involved in something they had no idea would effect them the way it did. This story is a composite of many ex-soldiers experiences in all our past conflicts. Blessings, blessings, blessings, for them. Signed Marcus Romanzo.

Americas Hope For It's Future.

Today this March 13, 2022 so hatefully divided from our own best interests for our future as American's and this country called America. Mostly because of the destruction coming from the Republican Parties extremist's far right wing conspiracy base. This is not in my opinion, anything recent like in the last four years of the Trump presidency it just got overwhelmingly strong because those far right wing conspiracy based extremist's know how to make up lies to destroy rational and reasonable thinking and discussion about anything going on in America. This destructive force goes back to before the twentieth century.

It has had "Peaks And troth's" in different decades of the twentieth century like the 1910s 1920s, 1930s, 1940s, 1950s. Slowed down a lot in the late 1950s because of the goodness of President Eisenhower. Peaked again in the late 1960s, the 1970s, especially the 1980s, 1990s to present because of talk radio, then television to now of course, that all powerful force called the internet "Social Media." You and I know who that is,

MARCUS ROMANZO'S BOOK OF LIFE LONG SHORT STORIES

ENCOURAGING EVERYONE TO WRITE THEIR SHORT STORIES TOO

MARCUS ROMANZO

Authors Innovation
1 Ivy Lane Wallington NJ
Wallington NJ. 07057

from a television network devoted to misinformation. To generally what is called Social Media. To a president who refused to accept that he was honestly defeated in November 2020. The fruits that the far right conspiracy talkers brought us. Was all those Crazy Devoted To Trump rioters on January 6th 2021, honestly believing they could prevent the certification of the 2020 election by taking it from the rightful winner Joe Biden and giving it to Donald Trump the loser. Fortunately they had no real chance to do that. But you and I can see that the power of "Believing," in what a cause wants to accomplish is all that really matters. For causes of "Good," we should be inspired. For causes of "Evil," we should be scared, not kidding ourselves anymore about what the "Enemy" wants to accomplish in our, "America." Our democratic constitutional republic "America."The overthrow of our current form of government, for a "My Supreme Leader," dictatorship. Think about how those Trump devotees did not understand that if they could have got the VP Mike Pence and all the senators and congress people from both parties out in front of our nations capital. Those "Patriot's" to save America lunatic "Saviors." Would have with joyous and hateful glee, picked the politicians from both parties. Including VP Mike Pence and joyfully executed them on the spot. If in their wildest fantasy's they could have believed, this is a day of righteous retribution for the cause of saving America.They would have instantly destroyed America's, and their own futures. Totally and Instantly" no hopes for an economic future at all. Publicly executing/ murdering those public officials in the eyes of the civilized world and giving Donald Trump the presidency. Would be the most outrageous act "Ever."What would have happened to America on January 6, 2021? "Understand," the shining light that was America would have been extinguished forever. America would no longer be a free country we would be in Donald Trump and his advisors mind's a dictatorship because Trump frequently said he admired most of the dictatorship's in the world. Our allies in the world would have instantly turned against us. The US Dollar the standard currency of the world would plunge to "Zero" never to rise above zero again. All of the financial markets in "America" would crash to Zero, never to rise above zero again. All the financial markets and economies of the world would crash into permanent depression. "That means America too." That is what "That is what the hero's for Trump," would have accomplished for themselves, Trump and every decent person and country in the world. Who Would Trump and his revolutionary followers blame next? I do not believe Trump or any of his followers could envision what I have just wrote about. I honestly believe Trump himself would think, after some very prolonged scolding from our allies. And 5 or 6 months of frightful shocks to world economies and scary stock market sell offs. That Trump would believe is a real estate and stock market buying opportunity. That the world would just have to accept him, as the American president. Who as the loser of the 2020 election. Took the presidency by force from the winner Joe Biden of the 2020 presidential election. In Donald Trump's flipped-ed way of thinking about everything. He would say, "Hey, After All, I Am The President Of America, "What"? What Mr Trump? You would have succeeded in destroying America and all the deceit countries in the world. Just like you destroyed every business venture you were involved with over your entire business venture life. That is "What,"? Mr Trump.

America's Tragic Loss by Assassination of The leaders Who could Have Saved America For A Better Future.

Making America a humane and justice based society for the great masses of people of all colors and economic levels to this very day could have happened. I was a ignorant young child from 1960 to 1968. My ignorance was, not knowing what was going on with the civil rights movement in America. And America's foreign policy ventures in southeast Asia. My ignorance of understanding America's foreign policy in south east Asia could have got me killed. Just unknowingly me volunteering to step right into the mess that was America's foreign policy at that time. That same situation happened to other young guys like me in my army basic training unit. The worst thing did happen as I learned in late July and August of 1969, two of the worst months for American soldier's killed and wounded in Vietnam. I was looking at a "LIFE," magazine multi page pictures and stories about it. I saw 5 fellow basic trainee's that I knew, "Killed." I was lucky looking back now that I got sent to The Republic Of South Korea. Nice clean safe duty with only the

DMZ being a place of possible trouble. Let us start with Lyndon Banes Johnson or LBJ as he was called.

Tragically LBJ the president handed the presidency by the bloody death of JFK in November 1963. Realized he needed to move boldly on social problems for all Americans, civil rights, poverty, to Medicare and he did move boldly on those policies and programs.At the same time he was like most of the Democrats and Republicans of that time. Fearful of communism taking over southeast Asia.Because of the fear of communism spreading in southeast Asia. The Democrat's and Republican's were united on stopping it. So LBJ was about to feed this huge underclass of whites, blacks, Latino's. Who needed all those civil right's and poverty programs. Fed into this big foreign policy mess called Vietnam. This well meaning move to stop an enemy to the free world. Because LBJ was a young man of WW2, and saw how America and our allies fought and defeated Nazi Germany and Japan. That young Americans would realize it was their turn to do for America what their fathers, mothers, uncles and aunts, and neighbors did for America in WW2. In 1964 to 1966 I think most young Americans went along unquestioning of what they were told to do. Let us start with the first important assassination of the 1960s. John F Kennedy, a lot of speculation about if he would have concluded early our escalating involvement in South Vietnam. Then after his murder in late November 1963. The conspiracy about why he was killed in Dallas, Texas in November 1963. The conspiracy goes like. Hateful Cuban exile fighters, along with the CIA, that JFK wanted to demote to nothing because he felt the CIA gave bad advice on the "Bay Of Pigs," attempt to over throw the Fidel Castro regime and made JFK look stupid. Along with Mafia Crime bosses who lost their hold on Cuba's Casino, adult sexual services, and drug dealing empire The Fidel Castro Regime, threw out the mafia. Embarrassing The Mafia crime bosses and making them blame JFK for their embarrassment. They also hated JFK's brother Attorney general Robert Kennedy for his relentless prosecutions of their fellow mafia associates. Basically the conspiracy goes they planned and plotted and waited until the right time and place came, Dallas, Texas. November 1963. If you want to see a very good film about the conspiracy of the murder of JFK. See the 1991 film by Oliver Stone called, "JFK." The second important assassination was

Martin Luther King Junior or MLK as he has come to be known. In early April 1968 in Memphis, Tennessee. Of course the horrible riots and destruction it caused. Was only half of how bad that was. The other half was and most important. "The loss of hope and direction," for everyone in the civil rights movement. If MLK had not been murdered. This leader MLK who was lead by a holey spiritual force. The command in his voice and use of words. Could have salvaged race and class divisions in America. Many disadvantaged whites, blacks, Latinos, all had the same problems. MLK was intelligent enough to know that, he knew it was not just blacks. That is why MLK worked for everyone. MLK his murder turned off the hope of any chance for America to save itself to become a humane and just country for all of us. I believe now we had to have MLK to live and not be murdered. To make us save ourselves from our bad natures. Sometimes in history one man is that important. Like Jesus was to the salvation for all of mankind. Imagine if Jesus had been killed by someone when he was 20 years old. Because that person thought he was a trouble maker who should be killed. What would have happened for mankind's salvation? Unless God would have resurrected him back to life after a crazed killer, killed him. We the mankind would have missed the salvation, we have a chance for today. Some people were that important in mankind's history. MLK needed to live, he could have saved us from our bad natures. He just was not resurrected.

The third most important assassination of the 1960s. Senator Robert Kennedy, killed while campaigning for the presidency in June of 1968 in a hotel kitchen by a young kitchen worker named Sirhan Sirhan a Palenstine christian. Because of Robert Kennedy's strong support for Israel. A lot was said by Sirhan Sirhan before his murder conviction and after it too.

He claimed he did not remember killing Senator Robert Kennedy. Looking back at Robert Kennedy's murder many thoughtful people of that time. Realized that just like Martin Luther King, that America had it's second chance at becoming a humane and justice based society for all colors and economic levels. EXTINGUISHED, possibly permanently.

"AGAIN," like Jesus The Savior. John Kennedy, Martin Luther King, Robert Kennedy. "They," needed to live and not die. Because their collective contributions to "Mankind's"

well being were just as important as "Jesus contribution was

to mankind's hope for salvation." What a horror-able thing to have happen to mankind's hope's. For equality, justice, peace

and prosperity at a rational, sense-able level for everyone.

Sincerely   Marcus   Romanzo Creator,   Savior,   Thinkers,   Philosophers,   Poets,   Song Writer's, Singers.

My understanding and opinions of some of the most well known thinkers/philosophers. Modern day poets and musical artists. Their good, bad, even angry intentions. Of their realizations about our creator, savior, and what is there to understand for us if we want to. "There Is No God." What many people have decided to realize, most are closet atheists because of the fear of sadness and possible hate they could receive. If they were to dump this on their family, friends, and business associates. When we had prayed sincerely for something and it seems like we did not get it. This has happened to us repeatedly, why? The conventional religions we grew up in, all told us from the time we were small children. We are Watched out for, father loves us, and when we pray to father he will give us what we think we must have at that moment. As we grow and see what really happens to us and others in everyday living. We learn what we were told cannot be true. Therefore father does not exist? Perhaps it is not father give me all the time. Perhaps it is father saying, you are complete. Look around at all the living around you. Participate in it and you will grow spiritually from it. Then you will realize, you have all you truly need. Instead of hating and beating up the conventional religion we were raised in. Because most of the anti religion hate in the world is based on the typical conventional religions we grew up in.

The leaders and teachers that only wanted to help us because this is what they believed in. What a shame, they did mean to do well by us. I can and did forgive my first Sunday school teacher. And my former church I started my spiritual journey in. "God Is Dead," a whole lot of interesting thinking from the 1900 century thinker. Friedrich Nietzsche. The other side of free thought, the mind control authoritarian types who have shamed us over the centuries into believing that we are not worthy of a gods love. Has it made us be better human beings to each other and grown us spiritually? Plenty of recent poet/song writer singers who I enjoy reading the lyrics to their songs on the internet. "There is no Jesus coming out of the sky, now that I know it I know I can cry I, I found out." "God is a concept by which we measure our pain." "Charlie stole the handle and the train it won't stop going, no it won't slow down. No way to slow down." My favorite thinker poet/ song writer singer from that era. "I am iron man, has he lost his mind, can he see or is he blind, can he walk at all or if he moves will he fall. Is he alive or dead has he thoughts within his head, we'll just pass him there, why should we even care." Two passages from the beginning of that song. The deeply troubled and conflicted views by the poet singer about his savior. Wow, is that not wonderful. "Cancel my subscription to the resurrection. Take my credentials to the house of detention." "No eternal reward can forgive us now for, forsaking the dawn." I am happy and a little more spiritually grown now at 72. When I wrote this at age 64 in 2013 when I felt I was growing some spiritually. That as long as I did. I would not fear poverty, illness, injury, or death. I am not rich, tough, or strong. Spiritual growth comes slowly it seems, but I now know I believe in it for me and all my fellow mankind. Credits to the poet/ singers, John Lennon, Jethro Tull, Black Sabbath, The Doors.

Sincerely Marcus Romanzo.

Dimensions

A women I knew in the early 1990s she was nice but had many personal problems. Her father helped and supported her, I hope she turned out alright it is now 2021. She told me she was a heroin addict sometimes in the 1970s. She had overdosed and some one took her to a hospital emergency room. She said while lying on the table on her back, she was moving up to something on the ceiling that was bright. Then she woke up from her care because the doctor had saved her from her over dose. But her experience made her see that there is more to this life then she knew before. I was very interested in what she told me, I started to think about dimensions. That maybe the entry to heavens waiting room is a dimension and that our death experience triggers the opening of that dimension door. Today because of modern medical advancement police, medical tech's, firemen, carry narcan with them and save people's lives on the spot all the time.

Dimensions

Like the images we thought we saw in a fog shrouded bank that was so real at the time. So may be the truth to what we call our world. "Dimensions." Will we advance to where we could flick the switches of our minds and travel the worlds that may be at the reach of our arms? Beings in other worlds or dimensions may be doing this now, there have always been a few among us over the ages who have said they have seen them, and met with them too. The term "Unidentified Phenomenon." It is wonderful to think that they are there somewhere. The fact that we could not get to Mars without arriving dead. The fact that our astronomers find places that seem like earth, but no travel ship we have could ever get us there. How could we get to those places? Have beings come from those places to here? The question, how did they do it? The answer may be "Dimensions." Think about looking up at the night sky you see all those stars some look close, the moon looks like you could touch it. Other stars are far away. We say wow, what a gigantic creation we live in. Yes it is gigantic it seems. The idea that our world is really a dimension is explained by looking at a silk scarf, you look at all the delicate weaving of the silk so small the individual weaves. That is what this eternity is that we are a part of. In our little weave or dimension we think we are in a giant place. And all the other weaves around us there dimension or world seems like a giant place too. I think that a handful of spiritually advanced people over the ages have traveled to other worlds or dimensions. Most of us cannot do this. Only a lot more time, centuries if not hundreds of thousands of years. That we would need to evolve enough spiritually to flick the switches of our minds and travel to worlds or dimensions that may be at the ends of the reaches of our arms.For us to do this we have to live long enough. To do that we have to value all of mankind's existence and our environment.

To do that we have to realize we are in a battle with our oldest and most basic natures. "Greed," and "Intolerance," which I think served us well once. For survival and advancement of our species. To control greed and intolerance for each other, we have to accept this as a starting point. For our lives and this world or dimension is a laboratory of learning and growing spiritually. I so hope we could be more then another experiment that failed. "Dimensions."

Sincerely Marcus Romanzo

Eldon And Burt, Two T Rex Buddies Near The End Of The Dinosaur Age.

Eldon and Burt, two T Rex buddies near the end of the dinosaur age. Eldon has the prototype brain for reasonable, rational, higher intelligence for the future of all creatures to come. Burt has the baser brain for all reptiles then and to now. Burt of course is forty percent larger then Eldon, all brute force muscle and terror. Eldon and Burt started their relationship with Burt warning Eldon to give up his territory to him or he will be torn to pieces. Eldon was able to reason Burt into not destroying him, instead being his watch out for all things in Burt's new territory. Because after all Burt would now have twice the territory to patrol. The victory of brain over brawn for Eldon. As they get to know each other, Eldon tries to engage Burt in discussion about the obvious changing climate conditions. Eldon has the ability to notice fine changes in the weather. He talks to Burt about his observations. Burt with great reassurance said "No don't you worry about it Eldon." We are T Rex the most powerful force of the hills and plains. We are going to romp and stomp and kill prey, rip the meat off their bones. Gorge ourselves on their meat , then gorge our selves some more. Don't you worry Eldon it will be T Rex that will rule forever. In the mean time somewhere in outer space. There is a large body of asteroids flying around aimlessly at fearfully fast speeds. Is earth where

some of them are headed? STAY TUNED. I would like
someone to make Eldon and Burt into a cartoon.
Sincerely Marcus Romanzo
Post story note. The mighty meat eating terror dinosaur's and non
meat eating dinosaur's. That walked this earth for millions of years.
Now we human beings have walked this earth for millions of years. Is
our ending coming too? Who
knows, but we may have the same vanity as T Rex Burt had.
Don't you worry it's going to be humans that will rule forever.

Sincerely Marcus Romanzo.

He's A Rebel.

This is a story about "Black Girl Group Music." How it affected me in the early 1960s in San Diego California. My visions for my idea for a television film only came to me in late life now. I am Marcus Romanzo, 72 years old. I go back to the late 1950s and early 1960s for my start of important rock and roll music. My place was San Diego California. My mother, me, and my two brothers drove from Columbus, Ga. In a, 1955 2door, 6 cylinder, 3 speed on the column Chevrolet station wagon. That was in June of 1960. My mother was going to try to reunite with my father and make our family whole again. Of course it was only to be for one year 1961. My father was a brilliant electrical engineer. A loving man to my mother and his three boys when he could be. But his violent impulses toward our mother, but never toward his three boys. Made my mother realize she had to get out of the marriage to the man she loved. A psychologist my mother and father were going to. After his examination of my father told my mother that without immediate care. My father could possibly kill her and get away with it. Because of his extreme mental illness. So in August of 1961 my mother filed for divorce from my father. I did not know it at that time that was very frightening for my mother. But my father said he would accept it and helped my mother buy a house in a middle class working area. Where we would live from August 1961 to July 1966. This is where the help that I needed would change me to grow from a severely introverted highly dysfunctional 12 year old boy. To a much more normal boy, thanks to the diversity of children living all around me. My brothers and I did not know it, but we were about to start a new life of discovery and freedom. I am sorry to say my brothers and I went our separate ways of discovery.

With our father out of our lives. He took a job with NASA in Greenland monitoring our space satellites. We could watch any television shows we liked and listen to rock and roll music on the radio. My father had forbid that music. I was discovering all the fine "Black Girl Groups." Their chart songs constantly on the radio. Influencing me to think and wonder what a love would be like for me. If I had the nerve to ask some girl. From "Do run, run," to "He's so fine," to "Be my baby." "The Crystals," "He's a rebel," to "Then he kissed me." Now I listen to all those songs on youtube.com

on Sunday when I can. My idea for a television film. I have an idea for a one or two hour television film. Based on "The Crystal's"song called "He's a rebel," listen to that song and see if it moves something in you. When I listen to it I can see those young junior high school kids. The girl describing his qualities. "See the way he walks down the street, that's the way he shuffles his feet. My he hold's his head up high when he goes walking by, he's my guy. When he holds my hand I'm so proud cause he's not just one of the crowd." Opening lyrics from"He's a rebel." Open the film with "The Crystals,"

"He's a rebel." The city is San Diego, California the year 1962. This is a young black couple both are 14 years old.

They go to a predominately black junior high school called

"Samuel Gompers Junior High School." They are both good looking, tall, and healthy. They dress appropriately for the

"In crowd," in their school. They are both on the outskirts of the "In crowd," in their school because of him. "He's a rebel," he is tall, strong, and lean. He is a track and wrestling star at his school. He needs these abilities to defend himself from the occasional trouble maker. Long before we called these kids nerds and geeks, they were "Book worms." What gets this young couple in trouble with their "In crowd," is. They are always together before school, during lunch, study hall and after school. He cares more about studying text books on electrical engineering and science. Then doing things his "In crowd" says are highly important. His girlfriend is always interested in what he studies and has her own interests in studying fashion design and business. They are just way ahead of everyone they know. The "In crowd" wants them to be like an "In crowd" couple. If you were young and your interests diverged so strongly away from almost every one you knew. You might have suffered for it and given up your individualism. Not this young couple. He went on to USC to study electrical engineering and gets a job with a small company at that time called INTEL. She goes on to USC to study fashion design and business management. She becomes important at VOGUE. The rock and roll from that era now moves me so much and that is why, "The crystals." "He's a rebel" now gives me visions of a young couple like in the song. Thank you from Marcus Romanzo.

Life, The Circle, And The Power Of Magic And Mystery

It is neither rising or falling, it is neither safe or in danger, it is neither good or evil. It is neither beginning or ending. What is it asked some in the group? It is life the person answered, next I will show you a circle. It is the symbol of eternal life. You cannot point out where the circle begins or where it ends. You are welcome to try though. That is why the person explains we have beliefs and philosophies going back to the beginnings of mankind. To the establish religions and philosophies of today. The person asked, do you believe in the power of magic and mystery? We are the power of magic and mystery. It is wonderful that we exist as we are.

Sincerely Marcus Romanzo.

True For Us.

Life is existence, and is the creative force of constant change. We are this, All that is pushing up against us, and goes through us but we do not feel it. Lying on our backs on a starry night, looking up into space. Looking any where it does not stop. Life is existence, and is the creative force of constant change.

Moe Dearest

This is my tribute to Curly Howard, Larry Fine, and Moe
Howard. "The Three Stooges," they did over 90. Three Stooges
Shorts from 1934 to 1946. I think I have seen most of Curly, Larry,
Moe, and Shemp, their shorts more then I can say. The pure style and
practiced professional care routinely done by them. With their style of
physical comedy, because they could have hurt each other if they did not.
I always enjoy the laughs in their shorts but as a former aspiring actor
who long ago stopped aspiring. I watch their delivery of their physical
comedy technique. "Wow," if anymore Three Stooges Shorts were being
made. This would be my writing contribution called "Moe Dearest."

Moe Dearest

Moe had a ten o'clock Monday morning appointment with
their talent agency. Their agencies name was Iye, Cheatem, &
Goode, Inc. Moe was to see agent Iye that morning to practice a gangster
crime script. Agent Iye went into the reception room to tell "Gorgeous
Molly," the gorgeous blonde receptionist. Moe would be arriving soon,
to get him some coffee and raspberry jelly filled doughnuts. Because
Moe loved them, agent Iye told Molly he was going to kill Moe that
morning. "OH MY," was Gorgeous Mollies reply. In comes Moe at
five minutes before ten. Hello my beautiful Molly, how are you on this
beautiful Monday
morning my dear? Molly said just fine Moe, agent Iye will be out
to see you soon. Have a nice cup of coffee and some raspberry jelly filled
doughnuts.Thank you my dear, I believe I will. Molly calls agent Iye on
the reception box to tell him Moe has arrived. Great, great, hi Moe I
know you can hear me take your time enjoy some coffee and doughnuts
I will be out in ten more minutes okay with you Moe? Sure Moe said.
Moe had a over sized raspberry jelly filled doughnut he made the typical
mistake of holding it at the top instead of the bottom. When he bit into
the top of the doughnut. All the jelly came out of the bottom and landed
on his chest suit pocket like a big bullet wound. Moe just laughed, then

agent Iye came out of his office and saw the raspberry stain on Moe's jacket that looked like a bullet wound. Agent Iye commented, hey Moe I see you are all prepared to go. Let's go in my office and get started. Sure Moe said, Moe and agent Iye went over the script together. Agent Iye told Moe a serious argument between two gangsters one gangster played by him agent Iye pulls out his gun and kills the other gangster played by Moe. Moe after being shot falls forward gripping his chest. So they start it off the loud argument between the two gangsters agent Iye does the shooting with a cap gun. Moe falls forward gripping his chest they finish the scene. Agent Iye said excellent Moe. Moe and agent Iye have finished their rehearsal, agent Iye tells Moe not to tell anyone about their rehearsal for this gangster part. Moe says okay, then asks agent Iye about the jelly mess on the floor.

And that he needed to clean the jelly off his hands and jacket. Agent Iye said use my office bathroom, I will ask Molly to call the janitor to clean up the mess on the rug. I will call you Moe when I know something so go out the hidden back way. There are gossip reporters watching this building. Molly has been out of the office running some errands, Molly is back now. Agent Iye calls Molly on the reception call box. Molly answers yes, come in my office Molly, she said right away. You see that red stain on the floor?Call the janitor to clean it up, and talk to no one about it. Yes agent Iye Molly said. Having some fun with Molly he says I took care of Moe he is gone and don't talk to anyone about that either.

Yes agent Iye Molly said.

Molly in distress worries she has been asked to cover up for a murder.

Then guess who calls the office?

It is Larry Fine,wanting to know if Moe is still at the office with agent Iye.

Molly says to Larry with worried seriousness Larry, Moe is gone. Okay says Larry, where did he go? No Larry, Moe is gone for good Molly says starting to cry. Molly says that she has to hang up for now. Larry quite surprised by what Molly told him calls out to Curly. Hey Curly I just had the strangest phone call with Molly at our agency. So what did she say Larry? Molly said Moe is gone, I asked her where? She said Moe is gone for good. That means he is dead Curly. "NO," Larry and Curly start screaming and crying, it just can't be not Moe. Dear sweet wonderful Moe, our Moe, our Moe Dearest. What are we going to do Curly? What about our act "The Three Stooges." In the mean time Moe has just arrived at the apartment lobby where they live. The front desk clerk greets Moe with a Good afternoon mister Howard is everything well today? Oh yes William every thing is fine. Shall I call your apartment to let mister Larry and Curly know you are on your way up? No William I want to surprise them, very good mister Howard. I hope you have a good afternoon sir. Moe gets to their apartment door, inside he hears loud talking and crying. "WHAT" he says, he listens to figure out they think he "MOE" is dead. Moe decides to enter quietly through the kitchen door to listen to this Carrying On, he kind of likes that Larry and Curly think he is dead. That way he can find out how they really feel about him, ha, ha, ha. Larry and Curly are still crying and now analyzing what to do next. You know Larry says to Curly we both owe him money we never told him about. So I guess now we don't have to pay him back Larry said. He is in Heaven now where you do not need money. Curly says at least we can hope Moe made it to heaven, maybe not? You know he was awful mean to us Larry, curly said, how about all the time. You can go down there for being to mean to your friends you know. Crying again together Larry and Curly say, Moe if you are down there we forgive you for being mean to us. We hope the man at the Pearly Gates will give you another chance if you ask him nicely. Moe having heard more then he could believe about his good and bad qualities, especially about forgiving him for his meanness to his two best friends. Comes out the the kitchen crying, seriously shocking Larry and Curly. Moe they said Gorgeous Molly told Larry that you were gone for good. I found out by listening to all of what you two guys said about me. I know now I have the two very best friends in the world. And I won't be mean to both of you any more. Except when we are play acting on the sets, do we have a deal guys? Yes Moe said Larry and Curly together. What about the money we owe you quipped Curly? Larry tried to stop Curly from saying it, then Moe said with sincere love in his voice all debts are paid for me. Wow said Larry we better call Gorgeous Molly at the agency and tell her Moe is alive and well. She will be so happy.

The End.

Post notes agent Iye is pronounced "I" I saw this agency or law firm name in one of The Three Stooges shorts. Eye,

Cheatem, & Goode. Think about what those words really mean. I cheat them and good. Ha, ha, ha.

Sincerely Marcus Romanzo.

The most ugly girl of my seventh grade bus.

This is a story about my seventh grade school year 1962 to 1963. I realized more then 30 years ago. That I was deeply saddened by what me and some boys did one afternoon on a mostly empty bus to a girl named Sally Swank. I wanted to be accepted by those boys because they were marginally accepted by "The In crowd," in our school. They use to pick on me so when they diverted their attention to somebody else to pick on, I was relieved. To try to get social acceptance from them, I joined in on the howls at Sally Swank, "Ugly, Sally Swank Is Ugly." We repeated those howls until she started crying, and continued them until we finally stopped. As far as I know Sally was crying until she got off the bus at her stop. I do not know if Sally ever rode that bus again. I will tell you now her parents should have contacted the school and demanded that we should be punished for our actions. I am sure Sally must have cried all the way to her house and when her mother saw her crying, and must have asked Sally what happened? No action was taken by the school, perhaps her mother and father took some action themselves. I said earlier that I am not sure I ever saw Sally on that bus again. After that afternoon of horror by me and those boys. Now to the point of this writing, I was being bullied by those boys. They turned their bully tactics on Sally. Sadly there is nothing new about children and even adults bullying each other. It seems to be a sad fact of life when it happens." Enlightening Hell's," as I call them. Your "Conscious" will demand maybe decades later that you deal with something you did. I was 13 when I joined in with those other boys on bulling Sally. In April 1963 it was not until 1989 or 1990. That this revelation hit me hard and I needed to accept my responsibility for being cruel to Sally. Fortunately I had been into consciousness raising since the 1970s. When it hit me so hard I cried. I knew that even if I could have apologized to Sally in 1990, That she could have had so much bitterness from that experience in 1963. That she could never forgive what me and those boys did to her. I know I may not be forgiven for what I did, I accept that. What is important for me was to accept what I did and not deny it. That way I could live saddened but truthfully with myself. And grow spiritually, there have been many more "Enlightening Hell's since 1989 and they keep coming all the time until the end of my life whenever that will be, I am 72 now. Because I am open now to accepting new revelations, it took me decades to learn this. I am not afraid to accept and deal with "New Enlightening Hell's," I wish well for all of us, when you get hit by your conscious for something you did in the past. Examine it and do not be afraid to deal with it, this is what your mind wants you to do. So that you will improve and grow humanely as a human being. Not just for yourself, but also for everyone important to you.

Sincerely Marcus Romanzo.

My Back Porch Spider

Do you remember "Charlotte's Web"? My back porch spider from my mid town Atlanta apartment in the late 1990's. I opened my back door one summer day and there he was. Most people would be upset and knock the spider and his web down. I marveled at his big web and he was almost as big as half of my hand. I say "HE" because there were not egg sacks in his web. He was in the middle of his web, he did not know he was daring birds to swoop down and eat him. He did aggressive bug control well into November. One November day I noticed he looked stiff, I touched him with a small stick he did not move. I realized he had died in the middle of his web. How glorious a way for a creature to die. He attached himself to the web he knew it was time to die. Isn't that amazing? I wish it was noble like that for us but we go along fearing death to the end.

Sincerely Marcus Romanzo

My Eight Grade Gym Class 1963 To 1964

" Gissellbrick," is how you spelled his name from my 8th grade gym class. A guy named Correo use to make fun of Gissellbrick. The way he looked. Correo was not hateful just silly but could border on being mean. Gissellbrick was a very tall and skinny guy with a bulb like nose and high kinky hair.

Around his eyes he looked like he was always crying. Probably eye irritation or a facial skin problem. In my gym class then, when you saw everybody in their skimpy gym outfits. A tank top and shorts white socks and sneakers. I felt so ashamed of my body because I had no muscle development yet and I was a little fat. I hated it when we had to be around the girls in their skimpy gym outfits. Correo did not make fun of me, and I walked home from school to his house many times. He would show me his model car collection and the projects he was working on. We got along well he never commented on poor Gissellbrick, only when gym class came every day. Correo would say hi to Gissellbrick in a funny way. Gissellbrick never teased him back he was much to quiet and sensitive. I know today in 2021even though the school year this year is far into May 20th and out. The kids go back in early August, when I was a boy in 1963 to 1964 we did not start back until after September Labor Day. Correo for me is worth remembering, he was the Mexican American guy who was popular with everyone.

(2)

I hope he turned out well, he probably should have been a stand up comic. I have special hopes to this day for Gissellbrick, Wayne Farmer a math and science genius. Kemper who's face and body looked like a swelled up red balloon. I hope everyone I knew then turned out well, even the people who did not like me and showed it. It is the same now as it was back then for boys and girls who have not so great looking bodies. When I see people in everyday life now, I see a lot of people of all ages with their physical problems. What I see to much of is extreme obesity, it has become a major problem in the last 30 plus years. I am always wishing blessings and help for them. Remembering Horace Mann Junior High School. San Diego, California, my 8th grade gym class 1963 to 1964.

Sincerely Marcus Romanzo

My Mothers, Mother, Lily Mae

My mothers mother was born in May 1901, I do not know what day. Her name was Lily Mae I do not know her maiden name either. Her first husband and father of my mother, her brother and sister. Was Paul Modling. They lived in rural Alabama. Lily Mae and Paul lived the very hard deprived life of the small farmer.After to many failed crop years in the late 1920's and early 1930's. Paul her husband gave up on trying to make a small farm work. He told Lily Mae he would be leaving her and the children soon because he was a failure. He told Lily Mae to go to live with her relatives in Columbus, Georgia. He shortly after telling her that bad news went out west like many people did who had failed lives in that time. Hoping for a new start. This sent Lily Mae into a crying and screaming panic right in front of her children. Lily Mae got herself together as best she could, she took herself and her children to Columbus, Ga. Outside of Fort Benning, Ga. To live with her relatives. After her relatives were able to clam Lily Mae down and assure her that she and the children would be alright. She became very helpful to them cooking good food, cleaning the house and washing every bodies clothes, apparently they were not very good at these tasks. Lily Mae would be able to find a job, and start to bring money home to help with the household expenses. This calmed Lily Mae down a lot and made her feel important, because she was helping out.

This was the early 1930's depression era to make things worse. My mother told me her mother was a very hard disciplinary because of all the depravity she suffered through. Yelling at her children's waste of any uneaten food on their plates. Frequently shouting and crying about the depravity she and the children had to go through in the past. I believe my grandmother was suffering from "PTSD," you can get it from many horrible personal experiences besides being in a "War." I could imagine my grandmothers relatives were strained by her extreme behavior. But they must have understood what happened to Lily Mae and Paul, and their huge failures as small farmers. They must have loved and prayed for Lily Mae to calm down and find peaceful ways to live. They assured Lily Mae when she had those fits that she is doing "Just Fine," what they did convincing her worked. Lily Mae's life did improve a lot in the coming years. She did meet a man who she loved and he loved her, they got married in 1938. He tried to help her, her children, and everyone else in the family. Everyone loved him and he loved everyone too. Sadly after a little over a year he got very sick and quickly died. This shocked and hurt Lily Mae, my mother, her brother and sister, and the whole family. It must have felt like a curse, my mothers brother started acting up so badly and getting in trouble. A Juvenile court judge gave him a choice of Juvenile prison or join the u s army. He took the army in 1940. My mother and her sister developed their own problems

They were both "Real Cuties," this gave them problems with meaner boy's who made constant rude sexual suggestions. My mother defending herself and her sister fought back sometimes against those boys. My mothers sister did get a boyfriend who was tough and he fought some of those boys and made them back down. Her sister had a guy who loved her and she loved him. This made it possible in 1942 for my mother to join the u s navy. Lily Mae saw all the trouble her children had after her husbands death in 1939.

Because of the support of her family and friends she did fine. In 1944 she would meet a man that would make her feel happy again. He was Major Edgar C Davis, U S Army, they got married in 1944. They stayed together until he died in July 1972. They had a great life after he retired from the army in 1946. They had bought five acres of land in the county off Macon Road in Columbus, Ga. They built a house, fenced off pastures for cattle. Raised Terrier dogs they had a huge chicken house with chickens, ducks, and geese. They had a huge garden, I am amazed at what they did thinking back about it. That little farm must have been carefully thought out. It must have been Edgar's life long dream to achieve if he could and he made it happen. Lily Mae and Edgar spent the 1940s, 1950s, 1960s right up to 1971. Raising and selling Terrier dogs, fresh from the hen house eggs, letting cattle graze in his pastures for a share of meat later. Lily Mae did not need to work, but she went to nursing school in 1959 to 1960 to become a LPN. She worked at the Medical Center in Columbus, Ga.

From 1960 to early 1971, she did retire from nursing and Lily Mae and Edgar slowed their lives down and lived out their lives together until Edgar died in July 1972. He got a very nice military funeral and was buried in the Fort Benning Cemetery.

Lily Mae had to adjust to life without Edgar, she still had dogs to raise and sell. A friend of Lily Mae and Edgar kept the big garden going for many more years. I now wish I had been involved in grandma's life but I was busy with my own life. My mother and her sister were the same way too. Lily Mae did not complain about anything that I knew of, she just carried on with her own doing's. All through the 1970s right up until 1981she took care of that massive five acres herself with friends who helped mainly keeping the front yard and pastures mowed. Gone was the big garden, the chickens, ducks, and geese. And all the Terrier dogs except for two kitchen dogs. When Edgar died in July 1972, he did not mean to leave behind a heavy burden for Lily Mae. Edgar and Lily Mae's dream in 1946 was to have a great little diverse farm. They made that happen, that is what truly matters. For many years nobody thought anything about that, there was no hand rail on the porch steps leading up to the kitchen door. Sadly it finally mattered in the summer of 1981. Lily Mae must have lost her balance climbing those steps and fell on the carport next to the kitchen porch. I heard she spent many hours on the driveway before somebody noticed her. After hip joint replacement surgery and months in a rehabilitation facility.

Lily Mae got to go home, she had to have a live in nurse to help her with almost everything.

Sadly dementia was taking her over and by 1983. My mothers sister took guardianship over Lily Mae's affairs.

She found a very high quality nursing home for Lily Mae. It was a private care facility not a county facility so all the costs

came out of Lily Mae and Edgar's savings. Janette and Dick Lily Mae's children and my mothers brother and sister contributed to the yearly costs at the nursing home. They had both done well in their financial lives and could. My mother Dick and Janette's sister could not help at all. The option to sell the five acre farm which had become very valuable since 1946 was always possible if needed. There is no way to reverse dementia on it's way to Alzheimer's, so Lily Mae lived out her life in that very good nursing home. She died in early October 1991 from a much to late to help case of pneumonia.

What a big funeral service she had, it was not planned to be big. The funeral notice in the newspaper because Lily Mae knew so many people over her lifetime. Made all those people come to her funeral. I met so many people that day when I told them I was Lily Mae's grandson. They told me I was very lucky to have her for a grandmother. Many people knew Edgar also. I realized I was very blessed that day and so was the rest of our family.

Notes

PTSD, means post traumatic stress disorder. Paul Modling

Lily Mae's former husband and the father of my mother her brother and sister. Did come back from his trials in Arizona and California in 1939 to live out his life with a new wife in Alabama and Columbus, Ga. Paul Modling died in early 1978, his wife Edna a Mormon by faith, lived until 1993. I had met both of them many times, they were good people.

My information on the life of Lily Mae came from my family of course. Thank you Marcus Romanzo.

My Mother And Fathers Marriage

What went wrong and when? How do you pick someone to make a life with that is going to be so "Bad," for you? My mother and father like anyone, like you and me want to find success in love with someone. When did the violence start in my mother and fathers marriage? Was there rage in my father that he could control and not physically touch my mother? Until he got to a point that the rage and the physical abuse went together? What did my father say after the very first time he physically abused my mother? Did my father say, I am sorry Paula I won't do that again. You know I love you Paula. My mother as the physically abused for the very first time. What did she say and do after the very first abuse? After dealing with the very first abuse shock, she probably said like you or I would. It's alright I know you love me Don and I love you. What do you say and do after the 10th or the 100th abuse? I suspect that if you are not going to leave the relationship. You say nothing. I never saw two people who were so harmonious when they were happy. Their happiness was not a put on to fool me and my brothers. The violence never happened in front of my brothers and me. When the violence happened between them it must have been very private. I never talked to my brothers about do you think mommy and daddy fight? The first time I knew there was trouble between them was when my father came in our room to sleep on the bottom bunk bed.

My mother came into our room with a 22 pistol we had in the house. Pointed it at my father and begged him to leave the house now.

He did and stayed at some friends of my mother and father Walt and Lois, my brothers and I use to play with their children. The police were not called by my mother about the pistol incident. That was in 1957, my mother and father must have had more violent incidents my father physically abusing my mother. Until September 1959 I was in my school class. A lady came in the class and took me to the main office. My father was there and he told me that we were going on a trip to Utica, NY where his parents lived. I did not question what my father said, I did not say where is mommy? We started on our trip to Utica, NY. I did not know if my father left my mother a note, called or anything. My mother could have called the Florida State Police and they could have stopped us. When I think back about that day now, I am sadly puzzled about so much.

We got to NY State visited NY city and the Empire State Building. We went on to Utica, NY. My brothers and I got to meet our fathers parents for the first and last time. Then on to Boston, Mass where my father had an electrical engineer job waiting for him at RCA. After four weeks my mother drove up to Boston from Cocoa Beach, Florida. My father found a rental house and our family moved in. We lived in Boston from October 1959 to February 1960. My mother and father would have another break up because of my fathers violence. She took me and my brothers by car to her home town in Columbus, Georgia.

Her parents and sister were there to help out. We lived right across the street from her mother and father. In late May of 1960 my mother and father were talking by phone about getting back together in San Diego, California. Traveling by car when we arrived in San Diego, we met my father at a popular Burger Restaurant at that time. We had their great Deluxe Hamburger plate. My father suddenly showed up at our table, sat down next to our mother. He said very seriously

after hugging and kissing our mother. He said how are you boy's? I have missed you very much, we all said we have missed you to, Daddy. After we left the restaurant we followed my father to an apartment. Where we would live from late June to late August. The furniture had arrived at the house my father found to rent. We moved in , in early September, so we could start school on time. My brothers and me all went to the same elementary school. I was 5th grade Steven was 3rd grade, and Dana was 2nd grade. My mother and father would begin another try at staying together and making our family work. It would end in August 1961, "Of Course," because of my fathers repeated violence to my mother. Which again was private between them and never in front of my brothers and me. One night I came home from a Boy Scout's meeting, my mothers dress was torn at the right shoulder and she was sitting on the sofa. Looking like she had been hit repeatedly. My mother had been able to get my father to go to a psychologist with her. The psychologist after his mental examination of my father advised my mother to separate from him.

Because the psychologist said that without immediate care my father could possibility kill her. A court would probably find him mentally ill and not prosecute him for murder. I did not know at my age of 12, how frightened my mother was to file for divorce from my father. Counselors know filing for divorce can be when a violent spouse could kill or seriously injure their spouse."My Father," accepted my mothers plea for him to leave. Maybe some calm and acceptance came over him and some special part of his love for her before the violence was there came through. I think about those possibilities often. My mother and father did divorce in August 1961. My father did help her find a house to buy in a middle working class neighborhood. My father would take a job with NASA in Greenland in early September 1961. My brothers and I had no idea how lost and alone our mother felt. She once was the wife of an electrical engineer with the prestige and high earnings. She had become a 14 year failed marriage, divorced woman with a established spouse support and monthly child support payment. She did not work, my mother came from that generation of women. Who were totally dependent on their husband's for support. I do not know if my mother turned to any of her and my father's friends for help and advice. I know my brothers and I heard many very late nights of crying in her closed door bedroom. I Marcus Romanzo, could write more pages about my mothers new divorce life. I will say that being married to my father and trying many times to stay in the marriage. I believe destroyed my mothers life. She tried going to San Diego State College, but stopped after less then a year. Then in May 1963 my mother had a mental break down and was hospitalized for two months. My brothers and I were put in Juvenile care, until she was ready to take custody of us in middle August 1963. My mother did not attempt another rising up from her troubles again. My mothers family in Columbus, Georgia, had been encouraging her to sell her house in San Diego and come back to Columbus, Ga. She did get the house sold and in July 1966 we drove back to Columbus, Ga. Sadly in conclusion even back home in Columbus, Ga. It did not help enough to fix the totally broken person that was my mother. My youngest brother Dana was killed in a gun accident inside our house. Boys playing carelessly with a small gun in March 1968, which was the final break that finished my mother. My mother died on March 7, 1990 in her house in her sleep.

Final.

I write this story about my mother and fathers marriage to let

those who read it to know. That violence in families is not unusual and if they had anything like my mother and father did. To please understand that situation thoroughly. You can hate your parents for the way they raised you. This is a terrible thing to say, but that was sadly the best they could do. Please forgive them if at all possible. Sincerely Marcus Romanzo.

Old Images, New Images

This is the first story I wrote in November 1998. Because of the conversations I was having with a young guy who worked at WTBS. He worked with Jane Fonda. He said try to write something and I wrote this "Old Images, New Images." This is a fictional story about a Charles Ritcher, serial killer executed on a dark cold winters day. In October 1938 at the age of 32 in the State of Illinois. Born again in April of 1956 in sunny southern California. I do hope this could be written into a 2 hour television film.

1st Old Image. Charles Ritcher strapped in a electric chair looking out through the head harness fearfully. A hood is dropped down over his face and then the sound of electrocution begins. Scene is non verbal. 1st New Image, forward to a hospital in sunny southern California in April 1956. A baby boy is born. 2nd Old Image. A growing toddler raised by a religious purity fanatic of a mother. Screaming to toddler about god's purity. The fact that we urinate, defecate, pass gas, excrete mucus from our nose and mouth. Is proof we have failed god. That when we do we should feel deeply ashamed. That we should never get any pleasure from touching ourselves, or should have thoughts of pleasure. As a small boy after being caught for touching himself in private areas as all small children do. Charles hands are tied out in front of him on a kitchen table fingers out stretched. Then hit with a wooden ruler until bloody.

Afterward mommy lovingly cleans his fingers and bandages them. Lovingly lecturing Charles on god's love and not to make mommy have to punish him again. And not to tell anybody about this punishment.

Charles will of course slip many more times again as he grows into young boyhood. Which costs him many more beatings with the ruler. Finally getting his scrotum branded with a hot kitchen fork by his mother. Afterwards mommy lovingly cleans and treats his burns, lecturing Charles on god's love and not making her have to do this again. And not to tell anyone about this punishment. As Charles grows into young boy hood his mother does not let him play with other children unless she is there to supervise. She tells Charles that he is pure and the other children are impure, but not to tell them that. She makes Charles dress in church suits all the time that smell like they have been sanitized. She tells Charles not to play like other children, or talk like they do. This causes Charles to be caught up in being an object of misguided anger and hate by the other children. This causes Charles to be beaten by the other children sometimes all of them at the same time. Charles mother never allows him to have toys or pets. Just religious articles like bibles, and crosses, and scripture scrolls. 3rd Old Image. Charles father is a plain short rotund man who is a mechanical engineer and mechanical repair meddling perfectionist. He takes any appliance in the house that works takes it to his repair bench in the garage. Takes it apart lays it out in order cleans the parts, writes out a blue print of everything and puts it back together. He subjects young

Charles to all these repair sessions with redundancy in cruel words and back of hand if he feels that Charles is not learning. Those sessions are where Charles will learn the mechanical skills he will need to begin injuring the children who beat and hurt him, and his first unintended killing. 4th
Old Image. Charles is a 13 year old boy who should be growing into puberty like any boy his age. Normal things like interests in girls his age has been stopped by his toddler and young boy abuse by his mother. Charles has been made non sexual. Because of the hate and beatings by the other children, he has become non social. Charles works at his fathers work bench learning how to repair everything you can imagine.
One day Charles father is teaching him how to repair the anchor bolt on his bikes brakes. He tells Charles that if the anchor bolt were to fall out when he peddles backward to stop

he would have no brakes. This gives Charles the idea about how to get back at all the children that had been cruel to him and beat him. Charles like most children his age ride a bike to school. He takes some assorted wrenches and a small hammer to school with him one day. He asks permission to go to the boys bathroom and study hall. The teacher says yes he may, he goes to the bicycle lot. To remove brake anchor

nuts and tap out the anchor bolts to where they will fall out easily. After doing all the bikes in the lot, he waits for the intended brake failure wrecks to happen. The reports start coming in of brake failure wrecks happening daily.

This gives Charles deep satisfaction and thrills knowing he will not be caught. One of the boys that was the most cruel to Charles was killed in his accident that makes Charles very happy. Charles realizes the accidents and injuries he could cause are unlimited. This sets him on a course of ever escalating accident setups, that for the rest of his teenage years would drive the thrill factor to greater risk taking.

Examples like removing stop signs at quiet intersections, putting clear grease on frequently used stairways at his school. Putting gear oil on a road so cars would lose steering and brake control. Bearing a spot on an electric cord so someone could be shocked. As Charles reached junior high school, then high school he took shop courses of all kinds. His accident setups he hopes to cause plenty of, fortunately few worked. 5th Old Image. Charles is 23, employed as a bookkeeper at a truck freight hauling company. He is an astute worker and learns to socialize with his co-workers.

Since he is no longer a boy who can be harassed and beaten any more, his co-workers do not know about his harsh past treatment. Charles finds some peace in his life for awhile.

But seeing the potential for accidents to happen on the loading dock in front of the office when trucks backup. Starts him thinking about how a accident could happen. It comes to him, a freight cart heavily loaded on the dock, if the brake was released and the cart started rolling. If it hit some one knocking them into the backup pit and the cart falls on top of them hurting or killing them that would be what Charles would want. The thrill rises in Charles and he leaves the office and goes out to the loading dock randomly walks by the freight carts and releases the brake on one. The cart starts rolling on it's own and causes the intended accident and death.

Charles carefully looks around and in the confusion moves back into the office he is at his desk sitting there in uncontrollable ecstasy thrilled. A secretary who is coming out of an inner office observes Charles unusual show of joy. But does not know yet about the horrible loading dock accident. Just then a dock worker busts into the office shouting the horrible news. The young secretary gets the horrible realization that this is the source of Charles joy. Charles does not know it yet some one has finally caught him. The next day in the office Charles hears the police have a secretary who may know who might have caused the accident.

That the police will be coming that afternoon to question her. Charles knows who the secretary is and is confronted with having to do his first direct killing and he does not have much time. Charles must think of a way to kill her, for the first time Charles feels fear and capture, not thrill and ecstasy. What should he do? Could he risk killing her on the company property? He decides to observe her from a distance and not let her see him. All the office workers get their one hour lunch at the same time, watching her go to her car Charles goes to his car stays back and follows her to a popular soda and drug store. Charles is going wild about what to do? It comes to him hide in her backseat area on the drivers side on the floor. He needs a weapon his belt he will try to strangle her with his belt. It would look like murder and robbery. Charles stays crushed down behind her back seat waiting for her to return. She does he listens for company pops up a little so he can see what she is doing. Looking at her face in a compact. He quickly brings the belt up and over her head and down around her neck and pulls down on it for all that he can. It works she stops struggling and is dead. Charles pops up a little to see if he attracted attention. Charles reaches between the front seats to get her purse finds money and takes it.

Then calmly as possible gets out of the drivers side passenger door and calmly walks toward his car. Belt less and ruffled he stops a distance away from the murder scene to refresh his appearance before going back to work. Then he feels a familiar feeling of thrill and ecstasy, Charles realizes he had never done anything this bold and risk taking. So now Charles had found a new found confidence to do what he knew he had to do next. Because Charles was never suspected for anything he did in the past there were no finger prints on him. This thrilled Charles and made him feel smart.

He knew the next two people he had to kill was his mother and father. 6th Old Image. That Saturday afternoon Charles makes his usual visit to his parents house, working with his father in the garage at his work bench. His father tells Charles that they need to go to the basement to adjust the lean to rich fuel mixture on the oil fired furnace. Charles father tells him that oil fired furnaces can easily get over rich and cause carbon monoxide poisoning and death. Charles has learned how he will kill them, simple, clean, and pleasant.

Sunday a week later Charles parents are found dead in their
beds when they failed to go to church or answer their door.

The deaths are ruled accidental. Charles inherits in their will his parents paid for house and all it's contents.

A $3000.00 life insurance policy. A savings account of $246.74. Charles is living well for a $27.00 a week book keeper. He moves out of the boarding house and into his parents house. He is lucky he has all these nice things because it is late October 1929.

Soon he and millions of Americans will lose jobs, cars, homes, and bank accounts as the great depression would take over the country. The deepening depression would also be a chance for Charles to kill more victims. Because poor people would be more willing to take a chance with a stranger. 7th Old Image. Spring 1930 the depression grows wider and deeper. Charles freight company closed owing him and all employees promised back pay they would never get. That does not trouble Charles, he has money, Two cars, a house, and plenty of food. So now he drives the streets of his city looking at all the new made poor everywhere. He sees desperation in the eyes of an "Apple Annie," on a corner trying to sell apples. The ragged exhausted young and older men with fear in their eyes and faces. Charles finds a frail weak looking prostitute that night drives to her alley where he finds it was so easy to smother her. He learns the frail weak looking people are easier to kill. Charles realizes his killing desire has to be well controlled and seldom done in the same area or he will get caught. Charles learns quickly not to solicit a woman who is in a group. Always find the solitary women far away from other prostitutes to keep from being identified.

This cautious pattern should have kept Charles from getting caught. He had just smothered and dumped a small prostitutes body in her alley that see worked out of. He did not know as he drove out of her alley and turned right onto the street. His victim had an associate who saw Charles in his car walked into her alley to check on her associate, because she used the same alley too. This lady discovers her associates body and runs to the nearest pay phone booth to call the police. She gets the police precinct near her tells them about her associates murder and the man and his car coming out of her alley. She waits for the police to arrive and for the next several days tells them everything she can remember about the man and his car. A few days later after careful investigation by the police. They go to Charles house confront him and arrest him. 8th Old Image. The detective on checking Charles into the jail house system makes him take off all his clothes to change into the jail house clothes. The detective is going through Charles clothes he takes Charles belt out of the pants looks it over and sees just below the buckle rivets the burned in letters CR.

The detective is hit hard with the memory of where he saw a belt with the burned in letters CR. The 1929 soda shop murder and robbery of a young secretary in her car, a belt like that was found around her neck with the burned in letters CR. That detective investigated that case and was furious that he could not find that murderer. He is furious again and wants to start beating Charles. Instead he composes himself calls in his fellow detectives tells them what he thinks has been discovered about Charles. They get the case file compare Charles just taken finger prints with the crime scene finger prints, including the finger prints on the belt. The detectives know they have Charles. It is finally over for Charles. On the re-investigation of the secretaries murder they learn that Charles and her worked for the same company.

The detectives learned that a bad accident had happened at the company. That the young secretary was going to tell the police that afternoon who she thought might have caused the accident. Then she turns up dead in her car that afternoon. Charles Ritcher was tried for the murder of the young secretary, and two prostitutes in late 1931.

Convicted on all counts and sentenced to death. He was also suspected in the loading dock accident and the death of his parents. When the police learned that his parents death came shortly after the death of the young secretary. The police checked back as far as they could about his high school, junior high school, and elementary school days. They found out about the freak bicycle brake accidents. Charles Ritcher was retired three times and finally executed on a cold dark winters day in October 1938, by the state of Illinois.

He was 32 years old. 2nd New Image. Sunny southern California 1977. A handsome healthy young man is looking in the mirror over his chest of draws brushing his hair into place. All around the outside of the mirror are pictures of his loving mother, father, sister, and brother. Pictures of him and his dog, pictures of him and his fiance at their prom. Many happy pictures and awards grace the bedroom walls of this young man's room.

He lays his just earned college degree on top of the chest of drawers and places the job offer next to his degree. His mother calls him from down stairs and tells him his fiance is here to pick him up. He yells okay, rushes to the bedroom door turns off the light and leaves the room. Panning the beautiful room the camera fixes on the mirror over the chest of drawers. Then the Old Images appear in the mirror side by side from left to right. First Charles the toddler, young boy Charles, 13 year old Charles. 23 year old Charles, Charles at the precinct house after his arrest. 32 year old Charles face peering out through the head harness before the hood is dropped down over his face. The mirror over the chest of drawers shows the horror of the man who was Charles Ritcher. The young man now with his great life cannot see this past in the mirror. What is important and matters now. Is the loving pictures that surround the outside of the mirror and adorn the walls of the room. Only love from others is what saves us from becoming a "Horror,"

like Charles Ritcher. THE END Sincerely Marcus Romanzo.

Our World

When I was a young boy in 1955. My family and I lived in Cocoa Beach, Florida. My father worked at Cape Canaveral on the launching into space and maintaining of our space satellite program. The area surrounding Cape Canaveral at that time was think plush jungle. My parents bought three acres of land near Cape Canaveral worked with a small contractor to build the foundation, block walls, plumbing. The inside framing, roofing and wiring. We moved in shortly after that, there was still plenty of work to do. My father always had Saturday and Sunday off, so he would work on the weekends to finish the inside and outside work still to do. My brothers and I would watch him work, sometimes he would hire a helper. A thick plush jungle that surrounded our house, had holes in the ground everywhere. When it would rain the holes would fill up with water, little worlds would emerge filled with tad poles and other creatures. It was beautiful, my father would work with cleaning fluids and spill some on the ground where he worked, I never noticed that until I happened to see one of these holes filled with water and tad poles. The tad poles and other creatures were floating on the surface of the water they were all dead. Decades later as a much matured adult I would say in the last 22 years. The importance of that dead tad pole hole holds importance to me now. I think it is a symbol of what could ultimately happen to our world. Although it sounds absurd I mean.

We have so much pristine untouched wilderness. We could not possibly poison ourselves to death, like my father poisoned the tad pole holes. "Could We?" I think this is why there is such difficulty selling this idea to so many people through out the world. That there is a climate crises, that we should do something about. Yet those in both camps of thought. Yes there is deadly climate crises, no there just could not be any deadly climate crises. Or just so little it would not matter much. We in both camps of thought all knew some place once that we treasured that has changed for the worse. Or is now gone. What will the earth be like 1000 years from now for people in that time? Just in case, should we try to do something for our 1000 years in the future fellow man kind and our future family members in our time now? I think both camps of thought would say yes. I would do something for our fellow mankind 1000 years from now. We as Americans more of us now are learning about how far back our family histories go to. In The Middle East, people on all sides of the conflict of "The Holly Land." They have knowledge of their families histories and cultures going well over 1000 years back. To us a 1000 years from now seems impossible to imagine. It is only time and it keeps moving forward.

Sincerely Marcus Romanzo.

Pattina Pawning To The Sea

Say of her name, I saw her by the shore. Walking alone with night to hide her face. Oh Pattina, Pattina pawning to the sea. Passion she sold conceiving not for birth. Pain in her life of love she's felt and lost. No way to save herself she climbs a distant hill. She tops it goes to the edge to pawn herself to the sea. Then like a bird in flight she flies out into the night sky. She plunges to the waiting sea and to her pain goodbye. This was a never made song by me in 1968.

The Argument To Not Kill Fredo Corleone

Poor Fredo his brain damaged as an infant by a virus and fever. No proper medical care for the poor who lived in those slums in NY city at that time. Mentally limited for life he did the jobs his father Vito and his brother Sonny would allow him to do. Poor Fredo was his fathers personal driver, he thought that nearly fatal day when his father was at an open market buying some apples everything was fine. Two men quickly approached the car and his father. Shooting Vito many times believing that would kill him. Poor Fredo panicked dropped his gun and all he could do was hold his father and cry. Fredo had the mind of a child you could tempt to do anything for candy. Later when The Corleone family moved to Nevada to control their Las Vegas hotel's and casino (2) interests.

Some very evil men who knew Fredo was a "Dummy" talked to him like you would tempt a child with candy. Fredo gave the security information about the Corleone family compound. After a huge party at the compound an attempt was made to kill Micheal Corleone that night. Poor Fredo figured out he had been used, he hoped Micheal would not find it out. Of course Micheal did, Micheal would not accept that Fredo had the mind of a child. Micheal ordered Fredo to be killed after their mother died. You do not kill a mentally disadvantaged person. Even though Godfather part two was fiction you do not kill your brother because he is mentally retarded. Fredo never should have been involved in Corleone family bussiness. Fredo should have been exiled some where to live in ignorant bliss for the rest of his life.Sincerely Marcus Romanzo.

Romanzo, Italians, And Americas Love For Mafia Stories.

Every time I type "Romanzo," spell check puts a red line under it. When you go to spell check for an explanation. It gives you all these words like Roman, Rome, Romano, Romanoff, Romero. No Romanzo because it is not a real name. My fathers family must have been nuts not to change it to something acceptable to Catholic and Protestant Anglo Saxon NY state America. But they did not and made a very good life for themselves in Utica, NY. My fathers grandfather came to America in the 1880's. His family were carpenters and house builders and did very well at it up through the late 1960's. When everyone either retired or died.

Most ethnic groups, Irish, Polish, Russians, Greeks, Chinese as examples. Did just like my fathers grandfather Italians did. They came to America to find freedom and prosperity by being honest and working hard. Now about Italians and their connection to the Mafia, the romance of the last 50 years. The Godfather, The Godfather part two, The Godfather part three. Good Fellows 1990, The Sopranos 1998 to 2008. Now revivals about young Tony Soprano. If I like it or not the Italian Americans are the most favorite organized crime group stories there are. Not the Irish, not the Polish, not the Russians, not the Greeks, or Chinese. It is us my fellow Italian Americans. Sincerely Marcus Romanzo.

September 11, 2001

This story about an individual on that horrible day is fiction. This could have happened on that day to someone who worked in those Twin

Towers. The point of this story is about an individual. That persons short comings and how it saved their life that day. I do not want to identify that person as a man or woman because that does not matter. In my past work life I am retired now at 72 years old. I have seen many people get fired from jobs simply because of being a little late to often. Here is the story. A person was on there way to work that morning, they had just come back from a week of suspension for being a habitual tardy. And what was that person doing that morning? Being late again on the day they were suppose to come back to work. Oh boy, this means being fired for sure. That person knew this and gave up on there hurried walk. And said oh well, might as well stop and get a coffee. That would take 10 minutes and then report in for the for sure firing that person knew would happen. Like many people that morning in that area who were inside and only heard the sounds of horror at first. Then went outside to actually see the horror taking place. That person saw the tower where that person worked hit like it was just floors below where that person worked. That person quickly realized that their problem with being late saved that persons life on that horrible morning. What ever else that person learned, should be life changing. Blessings for all who lost

(2)

their lives on that day. Sincerely Marcus Romanzo.

The Desperate Ghost On The Road.

I visited a small rural town. A quiet road not driven much anymore I found out later. Because time had past it's usefulness by. So as I drove farther down that road the pavement got worse with bushes growing up out of the cracks in the asphalt. I could see the deteriorating buildings. Houses,barns and little stores. I knew to stop, turn around and go back the way I came. That road was only going to get worse. Where I stopped to turn around the car lights shined on the buildings. As I made my u-turn something ran out of a building to get my attention and called out to stop for me, and help me please. I stopped and said, what is someone doing out here in this area? There is nothing here but abandoned buildings. But it is possible some one could be out here but how sad and all by themselves. I did stop it looked like a young boy or girl. It was a small woman. She was dressed in a long dark blue dress with a hood on it. She looked through my front passenger door window. Her face was dirty and desperate looking like she had not eaten in days. I said can I help you? She said to me with desperate need in her voice. Her face beautiful but distorted by some terrible stress. I did not know I was dealing with a ghost. She opened the passenger door got in my car and asked me to please drive. I did, I was lost for what to say then I asked her where I could take her? She said to her families house, and please just keep driving I said I will.

I drove on occasionally looking over at the side of her face, she was intentionally looking straight on. Like she would find her families house anytime. We got to a intersection that ended the terrible old abandoned road, I stopped at the stop sign. I looked to my right to see her, she was just looking down at the dashboard like she had lost interest in finding her families house. I said wanting very much to help. Where to now? She moved around in the seat opened the car door and ran off into the dark distance. Wait I said come back. I can help you. I could not see anything in the dark distance from my car. I drove ahead into what was the center of this little community. Looking for a police department, I found a small building with a police car parked in front of it. "Thank God," I said. I went to the office door looked inside a light was on at a desk. I knocked on the door insistently, I said hello, hello, a women needs help. Three or four times I said that until an officer came to the door. "Officer," I said a women needs help that I picked up on a bad abandoned road.

The officer asked me to describe her, I said she was small wearing a long dark blue dress with a hood on it. She was pretty but worn out looking. The officer asked me if I knew anything about ghosts or spirits? I said yes I have heard of them. The officer told me what I encountered was a spirit.

I asked him why? He told me in early November 1959. A wife and mother went berserk killed her husband and three children. Then after setting the house on fire making sure it was really burning down well. Killed herself with the same pump shot gun. The officer said he was baffled and deeply saddened because they were a prominent and important family at that time in 1959. They also were considered to be very happy too.

Worse then that, the officer told me she was his sister as he started to cry. I was shocked badly by what the officer just told me. I started crying and wrapped my arms around the officer. God bless you sir, may god help you and your troubled spirit sister. I know now sir I told him, like you I know spirits are real now. Where can I stay tonight officer? Straight ahead about a mile there is a lodge you can stay at. I will call them and tell them you are coming. I am officer John Bright, what is your name sir? Steve Perry, I am very pleased to meet you officer Bright. I went to the lodge eat, showered, and slept until midday. The lodge owner Charles was told about my experience by officer Bright. When I left at midday Charles said please come back to our little community again. I said I will Charles and I am going by officer Bright's office to say good bye. In the years to come I had found a small community of good honest people. Who all knew "The Desperate Ghost On The Road." Personally before her horrible tragedy. How nice to know people who believe in what most say is nonsense. In my later years I will retire to that community. I hope it can be revived.

Sincerely Marcus Romanzo.

NOTE:This story is fiction. I would like to see it made into a one hour television film.

The Littlest Gangster

My dear so very sweet mommy is dead now. Murdered in women's prison that she was serving time in for being an accomplice to murder. The gang that mommy and me ran around with in the early 1930's. In Kansas City and around the Kansas country side. Were called "The Five Guys Gang," My mommy's name was Betty, just like the Betty Boop cartoon character of the early 1930's. The trouble with my mommy was she was naive and innocent of how evil those men were. That we were running around with, those very evil men. They knew "What A Stupid Twist," as they called her she was. They did not know I heard them calling my mommy that. My mommy was not stupid. Her trouble was that she was like an innocent young girl. If you were a grown man and you met her. You would fall in instant love with her. My mommy was a 5 foot 4 inch super blonde stacked knock out of a woman. Instant "Hard Ons,"she said men would get, Ha, Ha, Ha. When she would hold them and talk sweet to them. My mommy could have been a movie star if she had been more lucky. The Five Guys Gang their specialty crime was breaking into stores late at night and the occasional poorly built bank. For all robberies they always cut the power line going into the electric meter. They had two black Ford 4 door sedans. They worked well planed and quickly pulled off robberies. Mommy and me were always with them on their robberies. We were told to stay low packed together in the back seat. Those robberies were always successful, no fights with store owners or the police. Never any gun fire.

Until of course that good fortune ended one late night General Store robbery. We were parked in an alley next to a General Store they had broken into. Mommy and I looked out of the alley and there was a cop car across the street from the store they where robbing. Danny the outside look out man at the front of the alley. Ran into the broken in door to tell everyone there was a cop car across the street from the store observing the flashlight activity in the store front window. That little town probably only had one or two Cop Cars and probably no Cop Car radios. Sure enough into the alley two cops came guns drawn, they saw the broken in door. They shouted into the door, this is the police come out with your hands up. No answer from The Five Guys Gang, the sound of a front door being broken open. The Five Guys Gang coming out of a front door, the two cops move to the front of the alley. The sound of a Thompson Sub machine gun being fired. The two cops try to run back down the alley and into the broken in door. Johnnie fires at them with his Thompson sub machine gun and quickly kills them both. He has also hit the car mommy and me were in disabling it's radiator. The Five Guys Gang would now be wanted for killing two policemen. No police authorities ever heard of The Five Guys Gang before that bad luck night for them. Everyone cursing Johnnie for killing the cops, You idiot Johnnie you know we never had to kill anyone before. Carl the gang leader said, and quickly raises his Thompson sub machine gun and quickly fires into Johnnie killing him. They grab everything put it in the other Black Ford 4 door sedan and we sped off. Nobody questioning Carl's decision to kill Johnnie.The trouble with Carl's decision to kill Johnnie was the police would use Johnnies body and the ford sedan to find out who he was.

And eventually Carl, Danny, Buster, and Clyde. The Five Guys Gang days were numbered now.We were out in the country on a two lane black top. Slow down, don't panic and turn on the headlights before we have an accident Carl Said to Danny. They were all very panicked but they had hours to get away. No one would find out about the two dead cops, and Johnnies body until early morning. The early 1930s depression left behind many little communities abandoned by the people who lost their homes, farms, and stores. There were plenty of places to hide out in. Carl picked a large barn as a place to hide the Ford in. There was a house next to the barn, we went into the house no electricity but dry goods were in the kitchen. A hand water pump that worked for fresh water. Carl said to Danny, Buster, and Clyde. With great fear and worry, you know Johnnies stupid act will get us all "The chair." The state police will be called in to find us. We don't have much time. Danny said we can hide out here Carl, don't you think? "No" Danny you dummy. The State Police will search every abandoned building from that store to here. They might even find us in a few more hours Carl said.

"Oh," I wish Johnnie had not been so quick to use that "Tommy Gun," We had a perfect robbery gig until last night, Carl said. Any ideas? Danny, Buster, Clyde? Carl said

let's see if there is any gasoline around here, gas up the car.

And make a run for it, there still may be time. Okay they all said let's start looking. Mommy and me were being totally ignored. Until I heard Clyde say to Carl, what about the twist and the boy Carl? Witnesses you know Carl. Carl with the humanity still left in him said to Clyde, we'll leave them here.

It can't make a difference in whether we all get "The Chair"

or not. I went into the kitchen quietly told mommy we got to try to get away now. Clyde was telling Carl he should think about killing us. Carl said no Clyde, but I think mommy Clyde wants to kill us. Quietly we went out the kitchen door and headed into the tall dead corn stalks. We were quietly moving as far away from that house as possible. We came upon a little stream of water went left and found a hole behind some large rocks to hide out in. A little while later Carl was calling out for mommy and me, repeatedly he called for us. The rest of the guys said to Carl, come on Carl let's go now. We are all scared to death of getting caught by The State Police. They piled into the Ford and got on the two lane black top, to try to get away if they could.Mommy and me stayed where we were for hours, I had no idea how long we stayed in that hole behind those big rocks. Eventually we heard sounds of men and they had dogs with them saying spread out men keep looking. Mommy said so happily it's the police son. We got out of our hole and called to them, they found us and asked us who were we? Mommy told them we were hiding out from a gang that wanted to kill us. We had great sympathy from the State Police Officers at first. Then on further questioning of my mommy, they realized we were

part of that gang. The State Police separated us, mommy and me did not know that was what they had done. We thought we would see each other soon. No, mommy was put in a detention facility in Kansas City, and I was put in a Juvenal

detention facility in Kansas City. Carl, Danny, Buster, and Clyde. Where all killed trying to run through a road block.

Thompson sub machine gunned to death in their car. It exploded on fire and crashed. The State Police had thompson sub machine guns too. Mommy had no lawyer to defend her, she copped a plea for accomplice to murder. Ten straight years to serve. Me, I was 10 and dubbed in the Juvenile detention center I would be in until my 18th birthday.

"The Littlest Gangster." I had such a sad and broken life, and my dear sweet wonderful mommy was murdered by other prisoners in her 2nd year of her prison sentence.

Sincerely Marcus Romanzo

Post Story To "The Littlest Gangster."

What is there to learn from this fictional story about criminals and high powered automatic weapons? What is there to learn from this story for average people like you and me? Who may only have a small hand gun? For "The Five Guys Gang ,"they upgraded from small hand guns. They had a well run trouble free robbery system that they never hand to use any guns before. Everyone in the gang upgraded to the Thompson sub machine gun with small hand guns as a back up. Wow, Wow, Wow, how much more macho inspired they all became . And Johnnie got to "Do The Macho," with his Tommy Gun as they were called back then. The average person like you and me today in our modern life. Threatening people at a public place we like to go to. More states now putting laws on the books for unlicensed, no permit needed, concealed weapon carry. Men and women too. Feeling more confident about that concealed hand gun we can carry now. Would we use that gun? Yes I am sorry to say. So we hit the bad person, then the bullet goes through that person and hits an innocent person. You and I would be held responsible for that. This is not a movie. You or I could be a Mall hero on there way to prison, for involuntary man

slaughter.

Word definitions, what is A Twist?

A whore, a prostitute, a dizzy broad, or dame. I will write a follow up story on the man who was. "The Littlest Gangster,"
his name Sonny "Boy" Joseph Williams.

Sincerely Marcus Romanzo

The Man, Who Was The Littlest Gangster

I am Sonny "Boy" Joseph Williams. Attorney at law, Criminal defense. How did I go from a 10 year old boy, dubbed "The Littlest Gangster?" To the tough criminal defense lawyer that I am now? Why is my middle name "Boy"? Because of my dear sweet wonderful mommy. She said I was the "Sonny Boy" sunshine of her life. I am the tough criminal defense lawyer that I am because my mommy was forced into a plea deal without advice from an attorney. Let us start with my mommy's case. She copped a plea to accomplice to murder. I found out at age 16 what the state police interrogated and terrified my mommy to confess to. The State Police Interrogators told my mommy that accomplice to murder was the same as pulling the trigger herself. That she would get "The Chair," and never get to see her son again. Unless she told them everything she knew about "The Five Guys Gang." That if she told them everything she knew about robbery jobs they committed. She would get visit's from her son while she was in prison. She did tell them everything she knew about every robbery job they did because she and I went on every job. She tried to tell the state police she and I never helped on any robberies.

The state police interrogators said like they "Cared." It's okay Betty we understand you just co-operate with us and you and your son will be together again probably in one year. I am sure that made my mommy very happy so she copped a plea to accomplice to murder. No attorney to help her when the judge looked at her plea deal with no recommendation for leniency from the state police interrogators. The judge told my mommy he hated "Gangsters" of any kind and sentenced her to 10 straight years to serve. Mommy started crying and begging the judge, the court officers just took her away to the detention block. Where she was later taken to a state prison to begin serving her time. Now my story about how I was abused by the Juvenal justice system. The officers in the detention facility kept asking me to tell them about why I was called the littlest gangster. I said I already told you my mommy and me never participated in any of the robberies we were just dumb enough to go along with that gang. When I went before the Juvenile court judge he looked at my file and saw only that I had been called the littlest gangster. That hardened the judge against me, and he said hold him in Juvenile detention until his 18th Birthday. No chance for me to have gotten a foster home. So now here I am, a tough criminal defense attorney my first job out of law school at KSU. Was the public defenders office in Kansas City, I was all ready to defend any one they assigned me. I did not know that the fix was in at the public defenders office. I quickly learned the public defenders office worked hand in hand with the police and the district attorney's office to convict every one who came through the public defenders office. I realized that the most flimsy of evidence was used to send everyone to prison for a long time and three people were sent to death row. Two men and one woman, I said to my boss. I cannot work for the public defenders office anymore.

Why my boss said? I just told him to keep him from black balling me in the law profession in Kansas City. I want to work for myself.

My boss even said good luck to me, I said thank you. I went right to work interviewing those people who I knew the public defenders office had abused with the district attorneys office and the police. In the months to come I would be re-litigating every case I knew was flimsy. I got all those cases thrown out for lack of sufficient evidence, and I got all three death penalty case's overturned. The two men were self defense, and the women was self defense from a husband who wanted to murder her. I really got my old public defender boss in trouble and the Kansas city district attorney. The Kansas news papers saw all the trouble I was making for the police, district attorney, and my old boss in the public defender's office. The newspapers printed the stories about the corruption between the public defenders office, the police and the district attorneys office. I am so proud of what I accomplished, My old boss, the district attorney , and many police went to prison. How about that? I am driven to this very day by the rage that burns in me from the injustice that got my mommy to agree to accomplice to murder.

Then she was murdered in women's prison. By some hardcore hateful lifer women. Who hated my mommy for her beauty, innocence, and sweetness. I am a famous criminal defense lawyer now, after the newspapers printed about what I had uncovered with the police the district attorney's office and the public defenders office. I became a hero in the legal profession, everyone wanting to hire me to defend their clients. The good people who needed my help. "And," the evil people too. And I knew who they where because of their client and the "Big Money," they offered me. I Sonny "Boy" Joseph Williams, does not defend corruption. Not gangsters, business men, or corrupt police, public defenders, or former district attorney's. Soon I would meet the woman who was like my mommy. Beautiful, innocent, and sweet.

She made me cry so hard when I told her about my mommy and me and our life experiences. We got married we had one boy and one girl. My Jenny pooh, and very young children, loved to go out in the country to picnic. There was a beautiful stream that we loved. I climbed up on a big rock over the stream and said. Hey Jenny pooh, Robbie, Jan, as I gestured upward with both arms to the heavens. "Made it mommy, top of the world." Just like James Cagney said in the best desperado gang film he ever made in 1948. Called "White Heat." If you love old B&W gangster films This is the best one.

Sincerely Marcus Romanzo

This story of course is fiction. I would like to see the littlest gangster. And the man who was the littlest gangster turned into 2 hour television films.

Comment: This story is an example of when people do not have legal counsel and some "So Called," sympathetic lawyer in the district attorney's office says you can cop a plea. You must have an attorney to give you advice or you could ruin your life.

The Spinning Globe, Chance, Hope, And Change

Many years back I was in a public library near where I lived. The had a special area for classic books of all kinds. They also had a large spinning globe. I had so much fun looking at all the places on the globe by turning it. And touching places on the globe without looking first. When I would look to see where I touched I would be surprised at the places I touched. It sparked a romantic notion in me that maybe I had a past connection to those places. So now here is my story. "The Spinning Globe, Chance, Hope, And Change."

The globe the base that supports it. The arch that connects it on opposite ends, so it can spin. We the watchers over time. That watch that globe for our ports of entry. Overtime our roles we had played. Well prepared now from our previous experiences. For our next entry point. Our role to play for Good or Evil, wittingly or unwittingly. To learn from our experiences, or refuse to. For happiness or unhappiness, so we will be generous or unnecessarily selfish and cruel. These things will make us feel fortunate or unfortunate. Example, "The poor old rich tycoon." We the watchers over time. With chance, with hope and change for the better. For the next time we arrive and start again.
Sincerely Marcus Romanzo.

The Truth About Me

The truth about me is I am constantly discovering new things to think about. In this hard to know what is true for me to count on life that I have. The thoughts keep coming and I keep having to think about them. Are we basically good? Or our we basically bad and should be left alone? The basic argument for democrat verses republican. I would say through out the world that we are 90 percent good. You can see it daily from small kindnesses we do for each other. To big kindnesses you hear about all the time. What I need now is honesty for myself and about us "The Mankind." Is there any hope for mankind as a whole? "YES," we seem sometimes to muddle along at an unlearned and dangerous pace, possibly self inflicted deadly.

Look at The Cuban Missile Crises of 1962. If one Russian submarine junior officer had not held off on adding his key to unlock the nuclear codes on broad his submarine. If fear of being attacked and lost communication with Moscow had taken over. We might not be here today to muddle along at an unlearned and dangerous pace, possibly self inflicted deadly. Amazing that we continue if such a thing is true. The Moody Blues said plenty about this in their song Melancholy Man. The close of the song, "That We're Going To Keep Growing Wait And See." We are slowly self correcting our courses in this world on all levels. Let's go over some of them. Individual you and I constantly, governmental and business very small around us immediately. To local, county, state, country, and world. All things can be fixed locally to world wide. Even though we "The Mankind," will in our best efforts and some of us in their worse efforts to wreck things continue on our separate ways. That seems to me to be the way life works.

All though it seems to be highly risky. I honestly believe other lives have come to our world or dimension. Because they are well advanced beyond where we are now. Because they know it is their universal duty to come here, to just see how we are doing. And maybe to save us from ourselves if the worse thing could happen to mankind and our world. Possibly self inflicted deadly. I do not know if that is true. Whatever is the truth about us is as long as mankind does not destroy itself. We will advance to where we could go to their dimensions or worlds to see what they have achieved. I am not talking about 20 years or even 1000 years from now. Tens of thousands of years or more may be needed for mankind to advance our mental growth to do these things. We are still not past the phase of "Muddle along at a unlearned and dangerous pace, possibly self inflicted deadly." Ideally we need to get past this phase. I think this can only be done individually then added up collectively. I can see that we as the highest species have a lot to do in the hundreds of thousands of years to come. I say "Mush on forward."

Sincerely Marcus Romanzo.

Extinguishment of our essence our soul, our being.

What becomes of us when our body dies? Does our soul, our essence our being go on to someplace else? Like we have been taught to believe. Those places are either very good or very bad. What if we just extinguish when our bodies die? It would be the most fair thing to happen to us all. Why do I say that? Because for the very best of the human beings who fear no place of eternal torment they die with a peaceful mind because they always worked for the betterment of mankind, it doesn't matter if they don't know that they just extinguish.For our fellow mankind who worked for evil from petty small interests to controlling the people of our world. If they believe in a after life, and believe any of the teachings of heaven or hell. Accepting a "Savior" to get into heaven instead of going to eternal damnation.

They hope their end of life vocally uttered acceptance of a savior. Will get them in that heaven with the good people. That will not work because what you truly are is exposed in your very being every moment you are alive on this earth. If the evil people can utter a phrase like "I accept you oh lord as my savior. The only sincerity they expressed in their life to save themselves from eternal damnation. Imagine if the evil people got to go to the same place the good people go to. They would immediately try to find ways to corrupt it and turn it into the evil that they are. Extinguishment of our essence, our soul, our being at death is the most fair thing for us all.

We all have some idea, faith based belief about what happens to us after we die. I am expressing one of them.

Life is existence and is the creative force of constant change. It is neither rising or falling, it is neither safe or endanger, it is neither good or evil, it is neither beginning or ending. It is life, the circle as an example, represents eternal life. Where does the circle begin and where does it end? You cannot point out those places a circle is a circle. But that has not kept mankind from trying, philosophies and religions from our very beginnings to established religions and philosophies of today. Are we safe in our existence? Yes, as safe as we can be at the moment. Good or evil, I believe mankind is basically affectionate and tolerant. Evil what we see in the world that is horror from small horrors to mankind wantingly extinguishing other people because of ideological beliefs. Evil does not exist as a label. Evil is when human minds descend into madness or what we would call insanity. What made Hitler, Joseph Stalin, Mao, Pall Pak of Cambodia or any of the human monsters from recent history be what they were and gain a following to control, command, and murder. Love by others that these human monsters of history never got as children. So they "GOT US."

Sincerely Marcus Romanzo.

The Song: Where Or When?

By Rodgers and Hart. I honestly believe this is a song about people finding each other again, in new times and new lives in our world.

"Where or when"? It seems like we stood and talked like this before. We looked at each other in the same way then. But I can't remember where or when? The clothes you're wearing are the clothes you wore. The smile you are smiling you were smiling then. But I can't remember were or when. Some things that happen for the first time seem to be happening again. And so it seems that we have met before and laughed before, and loved before. But who knows where or when." NOTE: The best version of this song in my opinion was by "Dion and the Belmont's," from 1959. You can find this song on youtube.com.

The words to the song "Where Or When." So beautiful to listen to by many singers over the many decades. What compelled Rodgers and Hart to write about such a strange subject to most people. Even weird and silly. Sure I remember my last life before this one. "No," I do not, therefore it must not be true "Past Lives." Is God, Jesus, UFO's, ghost's or spirit's true? I am sure most of us would say god and Jesus is true. Because we have been taught since we were small children by our family and church's that god and Jesus are true. That we are loved by god and Jesus that we should love god and Jesus and fear god and Jesus at the same time for our own good. Fear obviously never has worked on us humans. If we are going to be bad for ourselves and our fellow mankind some influence in our lives made us move toward evil instead of good. Belief, belief, what we believe in. God, Jesus, UFO's, ghost's, spirit's

past lives, future lives. Why did Rodgers and Hart make a song about such a unbelievable subject? Because we are wonderful human beings with great imaginations. And we love the art that comes from each other's minds. We always have, we always will. We are truly a mystery, why we exist at all? The circle is the symbol of eternal life meaning no beginning and no end. So why can't any of these ideas be possible? What is god we were taught? An eternal being just like the circle which is the symbol of eternal life. Neither having beginning or ending.

Sincerely Marcus Romanzo